HERE IN YOUR *Arms*

FORT HAVEN, BOOK 1

NICOLE HIGHLAND

Overall cover design: Nicole Highland – <u>NH Designs</u>

Cover image/models courtesy of:
Shutterstock   shutterstock.com

www.nicolehighlandwrites.com

ISBN: 979-868810 -678-7 (Paperback edition)

*Every once in a little while
someone comes along
that flips your world upside down
in all of the best ways.*

Shop the complete backlist today!
Visit nicolehighlandwrites.com!
Sweetest Love
THE COMPLETE TRILOGY
Nicole Highland
SOMETIMES LOVE DESERVES A SECOND CHANCE

Visit today!

Receive
Sweetest Kiss
for free when
you sign up!

<u>Sign up</u> today!

Before You Begin...

Ah, the teenage years.

They're full of angst, full of drama, and they're full of highs and lows. But above all else, they are filled with so many memories. Some are good, some are bad, some shape us in ways we never expected.

And, on rare occasions, they shape us forever.

This age group is one of my absolute favorites to write about, and my hope is that I've captured the essence of this in my story.

And of course, I hope you love Grayson and Sophia as much as I do.

So, if you're ready for an escape, let's dive right in!

XOX

Chapter
ONE

A blast of frigid air hit Sophia Hillcrest like a wall as she climbed out of her car with her hood over her head, protecting her from the icy chill. The month of January was always horrific this time of year in Fort Haven, but this one in particular…

It was one for the ages.

Not even the sun—if it actually had been *out* for once—would've been enough to soothe the bite of the wind as it howled, and though it was just cold enough to keep any major snowfall at bay, feather-light snowflakes drifted by as Sophia hoisted her bag over her shoulder and headed for the entrance. Her hands drifted to her pockets, desperately hoping to find her gloves, but as her fingers brushed against the empty space, she sighed.

So much for remembering to toss them back in there. She could practically kick herself in the ass for that.

A gust of wind kicked up, throwing her hood back, and she muttered under her breath, cursing the weather all the while. *Damn it all,* she thought. Why couldn't they have just lived somewhere nicer where the weather wasn't so shitty?

Her fingers, aching and numb from the wintry air against her skin, stiffened as she grabbed a fistful of faux fur trim and yanked the hood back over her head.

Pissed didn't even begin to cover how she was feeling. She hated this place. Hated the people.

And as soon as graduation rolled around, she'd be out of there in a New York minute.

Another gust of wind kicked up, knocking her hood off once more. "Why can't you just freaking stay in place?" she said through gritted teeth. She grabbed it again, holding it with a death grip as she kept it steady in place. At least she didn't have to deal with *that,* anymore.

But all the while she'd been messing with the damn thing, she hadn't been paying any attention to where she was going.

Or how dangerously close her feet were to the curb.

Pain splintered through her toes as her boot collided with the concrete, sending her spiraling to the ground. Her hands, still bitterly numb from the cold, splayed out before her as her palms scraped against the sidewalk.

"Damn it!" she hissed. Two female voices laughed in the distance, sending a wave of heat scorching her cheeks as embarrassment took hold. Leave it to her to wipe out in front of half the school.

Was it too much to ask to actually have a life that *wasn't* a disaster?

Sophia blew out a breath. Apparently, it was.

With her palms screaming in agony, she grasped feebly at the pavement, still reeling from the shock of making a complete idiot of herself in front of everyone. Falling down was always the easy part. But getting back up was the real challenge.

She froze, feeling the gentle touch of a hand on her back. Was she hallucinating? Was this hypothermia setting in?

Surely, this was all a dream. And a very, very strange one, at that.

"Are you okay?" an unfamiliar, masculine voice asked.

Sophia scrambled to her feet, nearly stumbling again as she turned to face the voice that had spoken to her. Her breath hitched. How was it humanly possible for someone to have such dark, piercing eyes?

Better yet, how was it possible that this guy went to Hardingdale? She hadn't seen him before. And she would've remembered.

Dear God, she would have remembered.

She would've remembered those dark, insanely gorgeous eyes. And she would've remembered that light smattering of freckles across his face. Yeah, she would've remembered him.

Every part of him.

"Um… yeah, thanks," she mumbled. "I think I'm fine."

The stranger gave her a half-smile and raised a thick, dark brow. "You sure?"

Sophia blinked, feeling a loss for words. He actually… *cared?*

Well, that was a novel concept for once.

At least, it was a novel concept considering how many assholes were running around Hardingale High.

"I… I think so. Although I'm pretty sure I must be in a parallel universe right now." Sophia held her hand to her face, feeling the heat rush to her cheeks once more. "I'm sorry. I'm babbling. Just ignore me."

The stranger smiled. "No worries," he said, smiling. "Just glad you're okay."

Sophia smoothed out her coat, feeling the full weight of surprise wash over her. Maybe it was the fact it had been so long since anyone bothered to notice her. Or maybe it was the fact that, for once, someone in this small little town was actually kind to her. But whatever the combination was, it was refreshing for a change.

Sophia's hands ached as she adjusted her purse strap on her shoulder, and she winced in pain, still feeling the sting of her raw skin.

"Are you sure you're okay?" he asked.

Sophia attempted to smile, but with her face still frozen, the effort was in vain. "I'll be fine. Just not the way I wanted to start my morning."

The guy nodded. "Sounds like you're having a worse morning than I am." He held open the glass door, letting Sophia escape the cold first.

"You don't have to do that for me, you know?"

"I know I don't have to," he said. "I just want to."

She didn't know how to respond. Kindness wasn't exactly plentiful in her corner of the universe, but here this stranger was, standing there as living proof that not every guy from Hardingdale sucked.

"You're new here, aren't you?" she asked. "I haven't seen you around here before."

He nodded, pulling his hood off his head, unfurling his dark hair. She couldn't help but stare at him. He was handsome. *Insanely* handsome, if she was being honest. And he was exactly the type of guy she could see herself falling for.

If she ever allowed herself to do that, that is.

"First day is today, actually," he said. "I'm Grayson, by the way. Grayson Cawthorne." He extended his hand, and from the moment their hands made contact, something inside Sophia came to life, melting her defenses. His hand, soft and warm against hers, was exactly the soothing comfort she needed on such a dreary winter morning.

And the kind of comfort she could easily get used to.

"Sophia Hillcrest," she replied. "Nice to meet you."

"Likewise," he said. "Yeah, my family just moved here. My mom's boyfriend got a job transfer."

That explained everything, she thought. Being the new guy, he hadn't had time to become completely jaded with this one-horse town. But give him a month or so and those rose-colored glasses would be off.

At least they would be if he was anything like *her*.

"Well, you're in for a real treat in this sleepy little town," she said sarcastically. "Everybody knows everybody's business around here, and they're not afraid to dig it up at a moment's notice."

"Speaking from personal experience, I take it?"

Sophia shrugged her shoulders. "I guess. I've always been an outcast, so that's my only 'claim to fame' around here."

Grayson smiled. He liked this girl. She was... blunt. Different. But not in a bad way. And if he was being honest with himself, he liked that.

A *lot*.

"Well, at least you only have until the end of the year to worry about this place," he said.

"Yep, and believe me, I am beyond happy about that." Sophia stopped just in front of her locker. "Well, thank you. For everything," she said. "It's nice to finally meet someone around here that isn't a complete dick."

Grayson threw her a wary look. "So, are people really that crappy around here?"

She let out a little half-hearted laugh. "I'll let you be the judge."

It wasn't until he looked up at the clock that Grayson realized he had only two minutes left to get to class. "I'm sorry," he said. "I should probably go. I gotta find my locker."

Sophia's heart sank. Between his kindness and that soft, doe-eyed look on his face, there was something about this guy she was beginning to like.

And *that* was a terrifying feeling.

Chapter

TWO

Cassie Shultz leaned against Sophia's locker, her eyes bright with excitement as she picked her best friend's brain. It wasn't every day someone hot strolled through the doors at Hardingdale, and if anyone would know the scoop, it would be Sophia. Of course, Sophia wasn't exactly Miss Socialite of the Year. Far from it.

But Sophia had the one advantage most everyone else didn't. She was an observer. The silent, fly-on-the-wall type that noticed everything but said nothing.

And she would've had to have been blind not to notice the newest member of their senior class.

Or dead.

"So, that new guy that just showed up… you wouldn't happen to know who he is, would you?" Cassie asked.

Sophia didn't even have to guess who Cassie was referring to. Grayson was the only member of the male species that anyone at Hardingdale High was talking about today.

She rolled her eyes playfully, ignoring her question. "Let me guess. You're into him, aren't you?"

"I mean, I'd be lying if I said I wasn't."

"Yeah, you and literally every other person here with ovaries."

Cassie's hands flew to her mouth to cover her laughter as she recovered. "All right, point taken," she said with a sigh. "Okay, so what do you think the odds of him asking me out are?"

Sophia closed her locker shut, leaning against it with faux exasperation. "Probably zero percent, if I'm being honest," she said. "I haven't seen him talk to hardly anyone today. But it could just be because it's his first day." Sophia shrugged her shoulders. "Who knows."

"You don't think he's hot, do you? Oh God, please tell me you're not interested in him, too!"

Sophia's lips pressed into a thin line. Of course, she was. She wasn't exactly blind, and he wasn't exactly hard on the eyes. But what did it matter? She'd bet every last dollar she had that he wouldn't be interested in her, so what was the point? It would be just another useless fantasy, one that would never become a reality no matter how much she wished it would.

It didn't matter that he was the literal embodiment of what she pictured her perfect guy would be like. He would never be interested.

Not in a million years.

"He's hot. But what's the point? We're going to be heading to college soon, Cass.

We'll have an entire campus filled with guys to pick from."

"But will we have a campus filled with guys that look like *that?*" Cassie teased. "I'm guessing we won't."

Sophia sighed. "Probably not. But guys like that are usually assholes, anyway." But, even as she said the words, she knew—to a small extent, anyway—that wasn't true. He had at least tried to help her up. And he held the door open for her. That had to count for *something*.

Right?

"True," Cassie sighed. "But who knows? Maybe he's actually a nice guy."

"Maybe," Sophia admitted. "I mean, he *did* open the door for me this morning, and that was right after he asked me if I was okay."

Cassie's eyes widened. "Why did he ask you if you were okay?"

Sophia sighed. "Because I tripped and fell on my ass on the sidewalk. He wanted to see if I was all right."

"So he's hot, *and* he's sweet," Cassie commented.

"Who knows? Could just be an act to get what he wants."

Cassie rolled her eyes, this time feeling a little less playful than before. "Oh my God, you are so negative. Do you *always* have to think the worst of every human being on the planet?"

Sophia shrugged. "Look around, Cass. I don't have to. They usually do a pretty good job proving it all by themselves."

Cassie threw her arm around Sophia's shoulder. "I know. But, you know, it's okay to take a leap of faith sometimes. Besides, if he really was an asshole, he wouldn't have bothered helping you up. He would've just left your ass on the ground."

She could deny it all she wanted, but Cassie was right. He could've just left her there and walked on by. But he didn't.

And *that* spoke volumes.

Cassie's words swirled inside Sophia's mind as she walked into class. Maybe

Cassie *did* have a point. Maybe she'd been jaded for so long that she wouldn't recognize a nice guy even if he was standing in front of her.

She sighed as she flopped her bag on the ground and took her seat. *He's just another guy*, she thought. *You know they all act the same.*

Except, something deep inside her knew he wasn't 'just another guy.'

If Sophia had to write on paper what her dream guy would be like, it would be him. She didn't intend for it to describe him to a T, but she couldn't help but notice that he checked all the boxes.

Her inner voice scoffed. She'd known him for what, all of a few hours or so? It wasn't as though she really *knew* him.

Not to mention, it was senior year. She wasn't planning on sticking around this messed up town after graduation. She'd be moving on to brighter and better things, preferably far, far away from Fort Haven.

So why bother fantasizing about him? Why bother wanting someone she knew full well she would never have?

Because you can't help it.

The thought was slightly alarming. But it didn't matter how many warm, fuzzy feelings she was starting to have for him. Guys like that didn't date girls like her. They didn't go for oddball, quirky girls that would rather spend a Friday night at home watching rom-coms than go out and party. They didn't go for girls that didn't give a crap about what they ate. They went for the girls with the perfect hair, the perfect bodies, and the ones that would rather starve themselves than stuff their faces with Oreos.

Yes, guys like Grayson would never be interested in girls like Sophia.

Oh well, she thought. *At least I'll be able to focus if he's not around.*

Her eyes flickered to the doorway as Mrs. Masterson spoke to someone in the doorway. She couldn't hear much from where she sat, but a moment later, the figure in the doorway came into view as clear as day. Sophia's heart rose to her throat.

Grayson.

Her white knight from earlier in the day was standing there, breathing in the same room she was in. She couldn't believe her eyes. She looked to her left, realizing the only remaining seat was the one next to her.

She *really* needed to get over him. But every time he glanced her way and those rich, dark eyes locked on hers, something deep within her chest stirred every time. Sure, she had a few crushes off and on over the last several years. But this…

This was… different. Stupidly unexplainable.

And certainly unexpected.

So, he had a handsome face, and he had a fleeting moment of kindness towards her. Big deal.

Except, it kinda *was* a big deal. At least to her. Not that *he* would ever be interested.

Or at least, that was what she would have to remind herself of every day for the rest of the semester where she'd be painfully reminded of how out of his league she was. And having to sit right next to him?

That was going to be pure torture. Blissful torture, but torture all the same.

Sophia pulled open her notebook and flipped to the first clean sheet of paper she could find. Maybe she would never tell him how she truly felt about him, but if she could distract herself from her own mind, so be it. So she did the one thing she always did when she needed to escape.

She wrote.

And her words would be her and her notebook's little secrets from now until eternity.

Her thoughts had all but drifted completely away from class as she glanced over at Grayson. He was writing furiously like it was the most exciting lecture he'd ever sat through.

Except it wasn't. At least, not to Sophia. Learning about the branches of government wasn't exactly the highlight of her day. But seeing Grayson?

That definitely was.

Not that she really wanted to admit it to herself. But damn. Those stupid, nagging thoughts just refused to go away, and the voice in her head refused to shut up. She would've given anything for them to just disappear.

At least then she might finally have some peace inside her mind.

"Miss Hillcrest!"

Sophia's head snapped back to attention. Somewhere between the first word she'd written and the last, she'd gotten lost in her own fantasies.

"I need you to get up to speed," Mrs. Masterson said. She held up her copy of the textbook. "Page 84, if you want to join the rest of us."

Wave upon wave of heated embarrassment flooded her cheeks. *Way to go,* she thought. *Could you make it any more obvious that you were in La-La-Land?*

"S-sorry," she stammered. "I was just… writing some notes."

Her cheeks reddened as Grayson's gaze washed over her. She didn't have to look fully in his direction to know he was staring right at her from across the aisle.

God, this day is already abysmal, she thought. How was she ever going to survive the rest of this semester with this kind of distraction?

Her thoughts snapped back to the present, only to drift away a minute or two later when her eyes wandered in Grayson's direction once more. He pulled out a stick of gum and popped it in his mouth, and the faint scent of peach drifted to her nose, making her mouth water. She didn't want to want him like she did.

But holy hell. What she wouldn't give to feel his lips against hers…

Enough, she thought. *Stop thinking about him and focus.* But her eyes were stuck to him like glue.

No matter how hard she tried to pry them away.

His eyes caught hers, and he threw her a slight grin, whispering to her in a voice that was nearly inaudible. "You want one?" he mouthed.

Sophia nodded, and Grayson tossed one in her direction, nearly missing her hands as held them up to catch it.

"I believe you already know that we don't chew gum in this class, Miss Hillcrest." Sophia froze like a deer in the headlights. "The two of you need to see me after class."

Sophia's cheeks reddened once more, this time to a hue that would've even a fire engine jealous. She didn't dare ask if the day could get any worse, because there was no sense in tempting fate, and if she were any more mortified, she would've liquified into a puddle, right there on the floor.

"Sorry, Mrs. Masterson."

With irritation beginning to set in, Mrs. Masterson grabbed a dry erase marker and scribbled furiously on the board. "Let's begin with naming the three branches of government, shall we? Can anyone name them?"

To Sophia's surprise, Grayson's hand shot in the air. So much for that 'new kid' shyness. He was diving right into the deep end.

"Yes, Mr. Cawthorne. You have the answer?"

"Legislative, executive, and judicial."

Sophia scanned the room. He might as well have announced that he would be operating a kissing booth with the way every female in the room was salivating over him. *Dear God,* she thought. *Wait until Cassie gets a load of this.*

"Correct," she said. "And today, we are going to more in-depth into all three, and we're going to discuss the people that make up each of the three branches."

Sophia stifled a yawn. *It could be worse,* she thought. *You could be in here without Grayson to stare at it.*

She almost laughed out loud at the thought. It was ridiculous to feel this way about a guy who was practically a complete stranger, but something in his eyes had a hold over her in a way she couldn't even begin to explain.

Mrs. Masterson asked another question, and Grayson's hand shot up once more. "Thank you, Mr. Cawthorne, but let's see if anyone else has anything to contribute." Her gaze scanned from one side of the room to another as the students sat in silence. They were frozen, either too bored, too tired, or too disinterested to bother caring.

"Well," she said, "seeing as no one else seems to have an answer, I might have to bump up our next quiz. Perhaps that will be enough to light a fire underneath you all."

An audible groan spread throughout the class, and a few students rolled their eyes in annoyance. For the rest of the period, Grayson sat quietly, keeping to himself. He wasn't there to make enemies. Yet, he couldn't shake the feeling that everyone thought he was nothing more than a show-off.

And then there was Sophia. Sophia, the gorgeous blonde with the quick wit and the no-bullshit attitude.

God, there was something about her that was driving him crazy already, but in the best of ways. He could only wish she'd feel the same in time.

Maybe he couldn't make the rest of them care about him.

But if he could make Sophia care, that was all he really needed.

Chapter
THREE

"You doing anything this afternoon?"

Sophia shut her locker door and zipped up her coat, dreading the long walk to her car. "Nope. Why?"

Cassie threw her a devilish grin. "Because I might have possibly spoken up for you and said you would come with Grayson and I to get coffee."

Sophia's eyes went wide as saucers. "And why exactly would you do that? We both just got our asses yelled at after class. I'm guessing the last person he wants to spend time with is me."

"You got *yelled* at? You never piss anyone off!"

Sophia let out a sarcastic laugh. "Well, apparently *today* I did. Mrs. Masterson thought I wasn't following along. And she was pissed Grayson gave me a stick of gum. That's literally all it was."

Cassie rolled her eyes. "Obviously she has a stick up her ass." She quickly changed the subject. "So, you're coming, right?"

"Why? So I can sit there and watch while you two make out?"

The words hit Cassie like a smack in the face. "Wow. You're jealous I said something to him first, aren't you?"

"Jealous? Of *what?* This imaginary relationship that you've cooked up in your mind?"

Which, in reality, was laughable considering how much Sophia's imagination had been running wild. Not that Cass would know. It was her little secret.

And one she didn't plan on divulging any time soon.

"Wow," Cass repeated. She shook her head. "You know, I never thought I'd see the day where *you* would be jealous of anybody. But it seems *that* day has finally arrived."

Sophia threw her hands in the air in defeat. "Okay, fine, I admit it. I'm a little jealous. But maybe I just thought it would be nice if someone actually liked *me* for once."

"And weren't you the same girl who said earlier that there wasn't any point in dating anyone right now?"

Sophia sighed. "Okay. Point taken. But I *am* entitled to change my mind, you know."

"One look at him and I think even some of the guys might change their minds," Cassie teased.

"Now we just have to hope he doesn't feel the same about them," Sophia laughed.

"I know, right? I'd hate to be out of the running already."

All hopes and dreams of running away with the new guy went flying out the window as Cassie sat completely bored out of her mind.

So much for any hope of excitement. The guy couldn't stop rambling about history and science. It didn't matter how easy he was on the eyes. He was a total snooze fest.

And at this point, getting a hangnail would probably be less torture than listening to him talk.

"You guys don't mind if I head out early, do you?" Cassie asked. "I forgot I have a test to study for."

Sophia shot her look, and Cassie mouthed the words *all yours* as she stood behind Grayson. Sophia breathed a sigh of relief. True, Cassie didn't even last a half-hour at Clem's, but at least Sophia could safely assume she would no longer be vying for Grayson's attention.

And thank God for that.

"You'll have to excuse her," Sophia said as soon as Cassie was out of earshot. "She can be kind of weird at times."

"Nah," Grayson said. He took another sip of his coffee. "I think she was just bored. I get it. It's history's not everyone's cup of tea." He laughed as he held up his cup. "Or coffee, in this case."

A slight flush colored Sophia's cheeks. God, it must've been obvious if even a perfect stranger had noticed how bored Cassie was. "Yeah, she's not very worldly, trust me."

"It's okay. Nothing wrong with that. We all have different interests."

The next two hours flew by in a blur as they sat at the table, smiling and laughing as though they'd known each other their entire lives. Grayson was easy to talk to, with a wit about him that kept her on her toes at times, but she loved it.

And she could've easily spent the rest of the evening talking to him if only they'd had the time.

"So, how did you become such a history buff?" Sophia finally asked. "Like, what got you interested?"

"Honestly, my grandpa's the one who got me hooked. He used to tell me stories about different events, even when I was a little kid." He took another long swig from his cup. "I remember being so fascinated with how other people in the world lived. And I just remember watching all those old war flicks with him. I always thought they were so cool. Plus, I come from a military family, so all of it kinda goes hand in hand. My grandpa served in three wars, and my uncle served in two."

Sophia looked surprised. This hadn't been what she was expecting at all. Not that she truly knew what to expect, to begin with. But to meet someone her age that felt this way definitely went against the grain.

In more ways than one.

"And you know what they say," he continued. "We're doomed to repeat history if we don't learn from it."

Somehow, even though she'd heard that phrase a thousand times, it sounded so poetic coming from him.

"You're absolutely right," Sophia said, raising her cup. "A toast for remembering history."

"Indeed," he said, tapping the cup against hers.

"Do you think you'll ever serve? In the military, I mean?"

Grayson took another long swig of his coffee, carefully forming his answer in his mind. He wanted to. And until today, he'd always planned on it. But now…

Everything had been turned upside down and flipped onto its head. He always thought he had a clear-cut plan of what he wanted to accomplish. But the waters were muddy now. He liked Sophia. *Really* liked her. And he wanted more. But whether their lives would run parallel with each other, or ultimately go in different directions, it was too soon to really tell.

And that made it a hard question to answer.

"I might. I haven't decided yet," he said solemnly. He finished draining the last of his coffee, then pulled out his phone to check the time. "Wow, I didn't realize how long we'd been here."

"Well, you know, time flies when you're having fun," she said, throwing him another smile.

Sophia's cheeks ached from smiling so much. It was almost terrifying to feel this happy. God only knew the last time she truly laughed and smiled.

But with Grayson, things were different.

He was easy to talk to. And intelligent.

And that was *definitely* something she could get on board with.

"Did you have to get going?" she asked, almost afraid of the answer.

"Only if you want to. My mom's pretty lax about what time I get home. As long as I'm back by midnight, she'll be fine."

Must be nice, Sophia thought. If she showed up back home at midnight, she would've been grounded for life.

"I should probably head home before too long," she said.

"No problem. I'll walk you to your car."

She practically let out an audible sigh. How could anyone be this sweet? Not to mention that smile of his…

It was damn near impossible *not* to fall for him. One more melty, heart-fluttering smile like that from him, and she'd probably end up in a puddle on the floor.

Walking side by side, Grayson's palm practically itched to take her hand in his, but instead, he shoved his hand in his pocket, resisting the temptation. Maybe in time, they'd get there.

But who really knew when that day would arrive?

"Well, this is it. My fabulous ride," she said, waving her arms in front of her old Dodge. "She's seen better days, but she still runs pretty well."

"Nice," he laughed. "Don't see too many Avengers around anymore."

"A lot of them had transmission problems, so that's probably why."

"Oddly specific." He eyed her curiously. "You into cars?"

Sophia nodded. "I guess you could say so. I'm not an expert on them, but I come from a car family, so I know a little bit."

His smile widened. He already had a list of things he liked about her, but this was just an extra bonus. "That's pretty awesome. I'm impressed."

Sophia flushed. "Well, thank you for walking me out here," she said. "And thank you for coming out here today."

Grayson smiled, despite the tangle of nerves coiled inside his stomach. Just the thought of her pressed up against him was sending adrenaline through his veins. Maybe it was selfish. But he wanted her. Every part of her. And in every single way.

And he could hardly wait to spend time with her again.

Chapter
FOUR

"Hey, are you free tonight?"

Sophia's heart did a little happy dance as she looked up to find Gray standing beside her locker. For once, she'd actually, maybe, possibly have something to look forward to on a Friday night.

And *that* was a pretty awesome feeling to have.

"You really have to ask?" she teased.

"Well, I mean, it's the nice thing to do. But yeah, I'm asking, anyway. Didn't know if you wanted to get together and study or not."

"But we don't have a quiz until next Friday, right?"

"All the more reason to take advantage of the time. Unless you think you've got this in the bag."

Sophia rolled her eyes. "Yeah, right. I'm not a history buff like you are. If anyone has this in the bag, it would be you."

"Hey, I do still study. Sometimes," he grinned. "So, what do you say?"

Sophia pondered it for a moment. "I'm game for it. My place or yours?"

"I thought maybe you could come over to my place."

There was a fifty-fifty chance her mom wouldn't be okay with it, but big deal. She could get over it. It was just studying, anyway.

Right?

"Uh, yeah, sure, that sounds good to me," she said. "Do you want to meet right after school?"

Sophia could see the wheels in his mind turning. "Not right after school. I am going to go visit my grandma. Maybe around six, instead? I'll take care of dinner."

Her heart fluttered in her chest. There he went again, being unbelievably sweet and cute. Sometimes it didn't even seem real. But she was a sucker for it, making her turn to a pile of mush every time. "You don't have to do that, you know."

"I don't *have* to, but I want to. I'm not gonna let you go hungry. Besides, who studies on an empty stomach?"

Sophia's stomach was a jumbled mess of nerves as she made the turn down County Road 40. Maybe it didn't seem like a big step to most, but going to Grayson's house was kind of a big deal. A *really* big deal.

Especially considering this would be the first time she'd be meeting his family.

Her eyes squinted at the windshield as she honed in on a car sitting on the side of the road. *Strange,* she thought. *Seems like a sketchy place to park.* Aside from the driver, the car was empty otherwise.

And if she didn't know any better, she would've sworn the driver was Steve Jensen.

Sophia rolled her eyes. She'd heard the rumors. God knew there were plenty surrounding him and his obsessive, stalker-ish ways. But surely, he wouldn't stoop as low as to hang out on back roads like some absolute creep.

Would he?

A shudder rolled through her. Neighbor or not, the guy was weird as hell.

With a shaky finger, Sophia pressed the doorbell and waited for Gray to appear. Butterflies fluttered in her stomach as the seconds ticked by, and seconds later Grayson emerged.

Her eyes scanned him from head to toe. His faded MGMT tee had certainly seen better days, but it fit him like a glove, clinging to his muscular body.

And holy hell, he looked good.

"Sorry, just got out of the shower." Somehow, even a bit messy, his hair still looked good. And she could just imagine what it would feel like to run her hands through it. She could picture it so clearly… they'd be lying there on a picnic blanket, gazing into each other's eyes…

Sophia snapped herself back to reality. She *had* to get out of her own head.

Even if she didn't want to.

"You can come on in," he said. He motioned for her to come inside. "Just be careful on this tile. It's a little slick sometimes. Oh, and um, I'm making pizza. I figured everyone loves it, so I thought that would be a safe bet."

"Are you using Pizza Palace's recipe?" she teased. "Because I'm gonna be pretty disappointed in you if you change it up."

Gray laughed and gave a slight shrug. "I mean, it will probably taste pretty close to theirs, but I'll let you be the judge."

With bright eyes and a cheerful smile, Tanya Cawthorne peeked out from the kitchen, eager to meet Sophia. She practically burst with excitement as she brought Sophia in for a quick hug.

"You must be Sophia! So glad to finally meet you."

"Thank you for the warm welcome."

"Oh, it's no trouble at all," Tanya said. "I made cookies, by the way, so help yourself!"

A slight flush trickled into Sophia's cheeks. "Wow, thanks. I don't know what to say!"

"Well, it's the least I could do." Tanya lowered her voice to a whisper. "Besides, you're the first girl he's ever brought home."

Now it was Grayson's turn to turn red. "Mom, please."

Tanya shook her head. "Oh, honey, it's nothing to be ashamed of." She turned to face Sophia, staring at her with adoration. "Make yourself at home, honey. If either of you needs me, I'll be upstairs."

Still riding a tidal wave of hope for her son, Tanya headed upstairs, feeling a little more cheerful than she had been only moments before.

"Mom's a little… excitable, I guess?" he offered.

Sophia shrugged off her coat, draping it over the back of the couch. "Yeah, but it's kinda cute. I like her already."

Good, he thought. Not that he could tell Sophia that just yet. Less than twenty-four hours ago Sophia Hillcrest wasn't even on his radar. But now that she was…

He desperately hoped he'd have a fighting chance.

Sophia lifted herself up onto the counter, letting her legs dangle over the edge. "Good idea, because I'm starving."

"Me too. I figured we'd eat first, and then we can go over everything," he said, pulling down two plates. Heat radiated throughout the kitchen as Gray opened the oven and pulled the pizza out.

"You sure you don't need help with anything?" she asked.

"Positive. But I appreciate the offer. It's the least I can do for you."

Sophia quirked a brow. "You know, you don't owe me anything."

"I know. But consider it a 'thank you' for not making me feel like a complete outcast."

Her heart squeezed in her chest. Was that really how he felt? Was this town so shitty that they'd turn up their nose to someone just because they were a stranger?

Yes, she thought. *You know how pathetic people can be around here.*

"Well, trust me. I know what it's like to be judged. I never want you to feel like you're unwelcome around here."

Gray took a step closer, feeling the magnetic pull between them grow stronger. Maybe he was losing his sanity, but for once he didn't care. Beneath that snarky armor of hers was a heart of pure gold. And he wanted her.

All of her.

"You could never make me feel unwelcome," he said. "I promise."

She leaned forward, wishing and waiting for his lips to meet hers, all the while ignoring the bells going off in her head. She barely knew him. Hardly knew him at all. But as the thought crept into her mind, her hands moved of their own volition, reaching for his. Time was all but frozen as they wondered who would make the first move, and she gave his hands a light squeeze, hoping the subtle cue would draw him in.

"You know, I should probably check on the pizza," he said.

Sophia glanced around him, eying it as it sat on the counter. "You already got it out," she said. She pointed to it. "See?"

"Shit. Yeah, I guess you're right. I forgot," he said sheepishly. "Guess it just kinda slipped my mind."

A slight flush colored his cheeks. He'd been so lost in his little world that he'd lost all sense of time.

And God help her, that awkwardness was the cutest damn thing she'd seen in a long time.

"It looks delicious," she said. "Hopefully it tastes as good as it looks."

Sophia's eyes lit up as Gray grabbed the pizza cutter, slicing through the dough with an ease that made it look like the easiest thing in the world. "You're like a pizza-cutting ninja," she laughed.

"I'd hope so. I've done this like twenty million times."

She smiled, feeling her heart flutter in her chest once more. "I'd say you have the magic touch when it comes to pizza."

"Thanks. I gotta say, I still think my grandma's recipe is even better, though."

She tilted her head in surprise. "Really?"

"Without a doubt."

With two pieces on each plate, they sat on the couch, momentarily silent as they ate. "You know," Sophia said, "I think it's really great how close you are to her. Every time you talk about her, you seem so happy."

Gray glanced down at his plate, and his smile began to fade. "She's really great. It's just hard watching her fade away like she is. It's gotten worse over the last few years."

She swiped a napkin across her mouth, praying he hadn't noticed how sloppy she'd been. "How so?"

Grayson exhaled a deep breath. Some days he could talk about it easier than others. But still, watching his grandmother fall apart at the seams wasn't easy. Opening up to virtual strangers wasn't easy, either.

But with Sophia, things were different. With her, he was an open book, begging to be read and explored.

"She's not as active as she used to be," he said. "I mean, she's still trying to get out and about, but it's getting harder. Plus, her memory isn't what it used to be, and her art isn't what it used to be, either."

"I didn't know she was an artist. That's awesome."

"Yeah, she's painted for as long as I can remember. She's amazing. I mean, she can paint up anything out of her mind. It's crazy."

"That's incredible. So what about your grandpa? Is he the creative type, too?"

A flicker of somberness flashed across his face. "He passed away when I was a kid. So, I never knew him, really."

An awkward silence filled the room as Sophia stared down at her plate. She would've given anything to erase what she'd just asked, but the damage was done. There was nothing left to do but move forward now. "I'm sorry. I probably shouldn't have asked. I didn't mean to make you feel uncomfortable," she said.

"No, it's okay. You had no way of knowing any of that." His thoughts trailed off. Being this open usually bothered him. But something felt different now.

Different. There went that word again, popping up into his mind. So many times that word had bounced around in his brain.

At least, ever since Sophia came into his life.

"I just wish I felt better about the situation with her," he lamented. "But her health has really been going down the tubes lately."

"Well," she said, reaching for her last slice, "I'm sorry to hear that. We went through the same thing with my grandma."

"I take it she's not here anymore?" he asked. He braced himself for the answer, hoping he hadn't just re-opened an old wound.

"No," she said softly. "She passed away a few years back."

"I'm sorry. That sucks."

Her eyes flitted around the room, wishing for any sort of distraction that would push the sobering moment away. Then, on the other side of the room, she found her salvation—a beautiful baby grand piano that had long since turned into a catch-all for random odds and ends.

"Do you play?" she asked, pointing to it.

"Actually, yeah. My grandma's the one who taught me. It's actually her piano, not ours. We're just keeping it for her since she's in assisted living, and it's a pretty small space."

The look on his face squeezed her heart in ways she didn't realize it could. "Well, I'm sure she knows it's in good hands. I think it's awesome that you play."

"Pretty sure you're the first girl that's ever thought that," he laughed.

Her eyes went wide. "Seriously? I think it's cool. Have you played it recently?"

"No, but if you want me to play something for you, I suppose I can." He flashed a wide smile, then got up to head over to the piano. "I'm a little rusty, though. But I think you'll like this piece. Just sit back and listen."

She leaned up against the piano, feeling a little wave of anticipation sweep through her. It wasn't every day she got treated to a private concert.

But she was definitely game for that.

"I'm not making you nervous, am I?"

Gray shook his head. "Nope, I'm just warming up."

Chapter

FIVE

"Sophia!"

Her head whipped around toward her neighbor's house. The voice *sounded* like Steve. It really did. But something just seemed… off. Like she couldn't quite put her finger on it.

And God, she prayed it wasn't. All she wanted to do was head inside and go to bed. But in the dim light from the streetlamp, it was almost impossible to tell as she squinted into the darkness.

"Steve?" she called. "Is that you?"

"Yeah, hey, can I come over and talk to you?"

His words were slurred like he'd just downed a fifth of vodka, and Sophia rolled her eyes, thankful he couldn't see the look of disgust on her face. God only knew what he wanted, but she was certain whatever it was wouldn't be important.

Not even a little.

"Uh, sure. I don't have a lot of time to talk, though."

Worry shadowed his face as he emerged from the darkness. "You still hanging out with that Cawthorne guy?"

She froze. How the hell did he even know that she and Grayson were speaking? And why was it any of his business what she did with her free time? Steve wasn't her personal keeper. Yet, there he was, standing there and grilling her like a damn drill sergeant.

"I am," she said cooly. "Is there a problem?"

Steve grimaced. Was she really that blind?

Or was she just playing stupid?

He swayed in the darkness, struggling to stay upright. "You could say that," he mumbled. "Been hearing some shit about him. Not sure he's the kind of guy you should be hanging around with."

"Oh, really?" she asked, letting the sarcasm drip from every syllable. "I'm sorry, I don't remember asking your drunken ass for advice. And no offense, but you're literally the *last* person I'd ever take relationship or friendship advice from."

He blew out a breath, feeling the irritation surging through him as he stood. "Look, I know you didn't, but… but just listen to me. Please." Steve fell to his knees, clasping his hands together. "Please. I care about you. I don't wanna see you get hurt."

"Hurt by *what?*" she snapped. "Look, I don't know what bullshit you think you've heard, but you don't get to dictate what goes on in my life. And you certainly don't get the right to tell me who to spend time with."

Her words had him seeing red. No matter what he did or said, he would never measure up in her eyes. He could stand there bleeding out, and she probably wouldn't notice.

Especially not if Grayson was around.

Grayson. Just thinking his name made Steve's skin crawl. Somehow, he had managed to get the attention of every living, breathing female at Hardingdale. He was Mister Perfect on every level, douche of all douches.

And certainly not good enough for Sophia.

"Then that's... your call," he said. "Just don't say I didn't warn you."

Chapter

SIX

Monday mornings sucked in general, but from the moment Sophia woke the next morning, Steve's stupid words were front and center once more, echoing through her mind like a haunting melody.

Just don't say I didn't warn you.

All weekend they'd been needling at her, making her question what was really going on. She could only hope Steve was wrong, that maybe he'd taken something out of context. But still, the seed had been planted, taking root and spreading the first inklings of fear throughout her heart.

Maybe Steve knew something she didn't. That was always a possibility.

But the red flags weren't there, and nothing Gray had done up to that point had set off any alarm bells.

She shook the thought from her head. Letting Steve's bullshit take up space in her mind rent-free was a complete waste of time.

And his jealousy wasn't her problem.

Jealousy, she thought. That had to be it. It was the only explanation. At least, it was the only reasonable one. He could've asked her out a long time ago, but he didn't. Not that it would've mattered. She still would've said 'no' to him, anyway.

It's not like she'd ever felt anything for him. Yeah, they were neighbors. Always had been. But other than seeing each other in passing, the connection just wasn't there. Nor would it ever be.

Especially now that Gray was in her life.

The drive to school was endless as her mind wandered, constantly thinking back to the weekend, and how good it felt to feel cared for. It didn't matter that Gray was the single reason she was still riding her high. It felt good to finally have something to look forward to again on a weekend.

And with any luck, she'd get to see him again the next weekend.

And every weekend after.

Sophia laughed silently to herself as she pulled into her parking space. No doubt, Cassie would have plenty to ask, and she'd want to know every nitty-gritty detail. But luckily for Sophia, there was nothing to report to her.

And even if there had been, some details were better left unsaid.

Sophia scanned the halls as she headed to her locker, hoping to catch Grayson before class began. Either Steve was a liar or is he was dead on the money. But one way or another, she needed answers. And the next time she saw Gray, she would get them.

Whether he liked it or not.

Cassie sighed in relief as Sophia approached. "Finally! I wasn't sure if you were coming today."

"Well, I'm here. Ready for another week, I guess."

Cassie eyed her suspiciously. "Everything okay? Or just a case of the Monday blahs?"

Sophia laughed. Mondays were always a drag. That was practically an unwritten rule. But that wasn't exactly
the *real* reason why she felt so out of sorts. "Well, I was having a great weekend until Steve cornered me about why I came home so late Friday night."

"*Steve?*" She wrinkled her nose. "Why does *he* care?"

Sophia rolled her eyes. "I think you know why. He's been trying to get with me forever. And now he's getting mad that I had a study date."

"How the hell did he even know you went anywhere?"

Sophia shrugged her shoulders. "I don't know. I'm assuming he was staring out the window like he always does."

A visible shudder shot through Cassie. "Ugh. That's so freaking weird. Oh well. He's an ass and you should just ignore him. There, case closed," she said, shutting her locker door. "So, tell me how your study date went!"

Sophia couldn't help the smile spreading across her face. "It went really well. Not that we got much studying done."

"Oh, really now?" Cassie waggled her eyebrows.

"It wasn't like *that*."

"So, let me get this straight. You two had a 'study date,' but you didn't study?"

Sophia threw her hands in the air. "I mean, yeah, I guess. We just… talked, really."

She threw her a look of disbelief. "And you expect me to believe that?" She let out a loud, hearty laugh. "Hanging out with someone that hot, and you expect me to believe you two were good little angels?"

Sophia gave her a playful slug to the arm. "Yes, believe it or not, nothing actually happened. Not even a kiss."

Cassie raked her hand through her hair. "Girl, you need to fix that the next time you see him."

Easier said than done, Sophia thought. If only she could.

"Well, if it's meant to happen, it will happen. Shit, we barely know each other."

Cassie stopped in front of her locker and leaned against it. "Like that's ever stopped anybody. I mean, you're into him, right?"

"Yeah. A lot. Maybe too much, honestly."

"Too much?" Cassie laughed. "Trust me, there's no such thing as too much."

But as her heart began to hammer in her chest, something deep within Sophia said otherwise. She was already swimming in the deep end, and this time, there might not be anything to hold on to if the waters got choppy. Her heart was on the line. And there was only one way to save it.

She'd have to stay away from him.

Even if her heart protested otherwise.

"But what if there *is* such a thing as too much?"

Cassie rolled her eyes. "There isn't. Trust me."

Says the girl who always wears her heart on her sleeve, Sophia thought. She'd lost count of all the times Cassie had her heart stomped on by a guy.

And that was exactly what Sophia wanted to avoid. No drama, no heartache, just happiness.

She sighed. Maybe that was too much to ask for.

Or, maybe, Gray's your guy. The thought flew across her mind at such an alarming rate that she froze in place.

"You okay?" Cassie asked. "You've got a weird look on your face."

"Yeah, I'm fine. Just… I don't know. Is it weird to be falling for a guy you barely know?"

"Not really. I mean, you can't help who you like. And come on. Look at him." Cassie pointed down the hall, watching as Grayson grabbed a book from his locker. "What's not to like?"

"The fact that he's into history and science," Sophia teased, practically bursting into laughter. "That's what *you* don't like."

"That's because that crap is boring as hell. I mean, who gives a shit about something that happened a hundred years ago? I don't."

Sophia shrugged her shoulders. "I mean, whatever floats your boat." She pulled her phone from her purse, cringing as she looked at the time. "Shit. I gotta go," she said. "Oh, and I can't hang out after school. I have to meet Grayson."

"*Again?*" A hint of jealousy swept through Cassie as she stood there, dumbfounded by her friend. How Sophia had managed to go from zero to sixty with Grayson was beyond her. But it was already starting to wear thin. *Very* thin. "You know, you *can* have a life outside of hanging out with him."

Sophia tensed, feeling the pressure beginning to squeeze at her. Maybe her instincts had been right. Maybe she was falling off into the deep end a little too fast.

And did she really want to be one of those girls, tripping over herself to keep his attention? After all, they were the same ones she and Cassie had laughed about behind their backs. And now, she was turning into one of them, falling for Gray at free-fall speed. It was crazy.

But the only thing crazier was the fact that, for once, she wasn't sure she cared.

Chapter
SEVEN

Sophia's eyes fluttered open as her phone vibrated on the nightstand. God only knew who would be texting this early in the morning, but whoever it was needed a swift kick to the head. It was only six-thirty, for crying out loud. What could possibly have been that important?

She rolled over, half-awake as she squinted at the screen. Even on the lowest setting, the brightness of the screen was mind-numbing this early, practically rendering her brain useless until the name on the display snapped her out of her haze.

Gray.

Well, he was certainly worth being woken up for, at least. She flipped open the text, feeling a sense of curiosity running through her veins.

Found out I don't have to work tonight. Up for another study date?

Sophia smiled to herself. Would there ever be any other answer besides a resounding *'yes?'*

Fully wide awake, she texted him back with excitement, practically counting the minutes until she'd see him at school.

Um, yes. :) My place this time?

His mom had been incredibly gracious last time, but it was only fair to ask. Maybe with any luck, they could bounce back and forth every other time.

At least, as long as he wanted to see her. It was only a matter of time before he'd leave, just like the rest.

She brushed the thought aside. Now wasn't the time to worry. Now was the time to enjoy the ride, no matter how long it lasted. That was what senior year was all about, anyway.

Right?

For now, all she needed to focus on was getting ready for class.

That, and wait for four o'clock to roll around.

Grayson pulled in behind Sophia and waited for her to get out. So many thoughts raced through Grayson's mind as he fumbled with his car door and stepped outside, and for once, the chill in the air felt good as it breezed past his skin. With his stomach practically doing somersaults inside him, he was an absolute wreck.

And if he didn't calm down now, he'd have no chance of impressing her parents.

So much for playing it cool, he thought. Then again, who was he kidding? Like he could ever possibly play it cool when so much

was riding on this moment. He wanted—
no, *needed*—them to like him.

But you're just friends, he thought. Yeah,
they were just friends.

For now.

But maybe someday, in the not-so-distant
future, they could be something more.

"You ready?" Sophia asked.

Grayson threw her a wry smile. "I think.
Not gonna lie, I'm kinda nervous, though."

Sophia patted his arm, sending a wave of
warmth through his veins. All it took was a
single touch to send him into the next galaxy.

And that was just the beginning.

"Don't be," she said. "You'll be fine. Trust
me."

From the moment Grayson entered the
living room, Dana Hillcrest's eyes honed in on
him with curiosity as he stood by Sophia's
side.

"Mrs. Hillcrest," he said, offering his hand,
"Grayson Cawthorne. Very nice to meet you."

Dana looked to Sophia, then back to
Grayson, beaming with happiness. "Nice to

meet you too, Grayson. Can I get you something to drink?"

Grayson shook his head. "No, but thank you, though."

"We're gonna head upstairs to study," Sophia said. "If that's all right?"

Her mother's smile didn't quite reach her eyes, as though a veil of caution held her back. "That's fine. I'll leave you two alone." She turned to walk away, then stopped mid-step. "Oh, and Sophia," her mother called. Sophia turned, half-afraid of what she might say. "Make sure your door isn't closed."

Sophia stifled a groan. "Okay, Mom."

And there it was. She figured her mother's inner 'helicopter parent' would kick in eventually. But still. It was embarrassing. Mortifying, even.

And how many other people in her class had to deal with this crap?

She heaved a sigh as soon as they were out of earshot. "I'm so sorry. My parents are just…"

"Protective?" Gray offered. "It's cool. I get it."

He… *got it?* Since when did any high school guy with a pulse understand protective parents?

God, Grayson was such a dream.

"You sure?" she asked.

"Yeah. I mean, they don't know me, and it's always a guessing game when you meet someone for the first time."

Still not convinced, she sighed in exasperation. "Yeah, but it's not fair to you."

"It's all right. Just give them time."

She rolled her eyes. She'd given them plenty of time to loosen the reins, but that still hadn't happened yet.

And how much longer was she expected to wait?

"Well, this is it," she said, flicking the light on in her room. "My little corner of the universe."

Grayson's eyes scanned the room, taking in the photographs and paintings scattered all over the walls. She had to have spent weeks, maybe even months on it all, and he could practically feel the energy and emotion coming from the walls.

The words escaped his mouth before he had a chance to stop them. "You're amazing. I mean, what I meant to say was... well, not that you're not amazing, but—"

Sophia laughed. "I know what you meant. And thank you," she said, smiling. "I know a lot of it's abstract, and most people don't get abstract art, so it's nice to hear something good for a change."

Grayson smiled. "You should be proud. I mean, you've worked your ass off. You deserve it."

A warm flush crept into Sophia's cheeks. "Thanks," she beamed. "Come downstairs with me. I wanna show you something."

With his curiosity piqued, Grayson followed closely behind Sophia as they headed back downstairs.

"This way," she said. "We're heading down to the basement."

Grayson looked up, noticing Dana's watchful eye as the two rounded the corner to head downstairs. Even if he had to watch his step for a while around her, so be it.

He already knew in his heart that Sophia was worth every effort.

Grayson's eyes didn't even know where to look first. Between the endless array of paint in every shade and brushes in every possible shape and size, it was like being in a full-blown Manhattan art studio.

Well, minus the skyline view, at least.

"You have your own studio down here?"

Sophia nodded in excitement. "Hell yes. One of the perks to being an only child and having a basement that my parents really didn't have any use for. So yeah, it's pretty much my domain." She laughed as she looked at the old exercise equipment in the far corner. "Well, except for some of that crap, which never gets used."

"So how long have you been working on this?" Grayson said, motioning to the expansive canvas on the floor. With its endless sea of red and pink roses, it was like a flashing neon sign, commanding the attention it deserved, and he stood speechless for a moment, trying to find the right words to say.

Beautiful didn't quite cut it. But it was the only word that came to mind.

Or at least, it was the only word that remotely came close to describing it.

"About a year or so, I think. It's forever a work in progress, I guess." A wide grin spread across her face as a plan emerged in her mind. "Wanna help?"

He stared at her in complete shock. *Did she just ask me to help?* "Me?" he asked.

"No, the ghost standing behind you," she laughed. "Yes, *you!*"

"I'm not a painter," he said. "My grandma is. But I'm not."

"So? It'll be fun."

"But what if I mess something up? I mean, how many hours have you spent on this? Hundreds?"

Sophia shook her head. "Don't worry about it. It's just something I enjoy doing. And you never know. You might just find that you love painting once you start getting into it."

Grayson stared at the table in front of them, unsure of where to start. "I take it you've used these two a lot?" He held up the brushes, half-laughing at how sad and disheveled they looked.

"Don't pick on them!" she teased. "I've had them forever."

"Yeah, but one of these days you're gonna have to get some new ones."

She shrugged her shoulders. "Eh, someday, I guess." She dipped her brush into the dark red paint, swirling and swirling until she had just the right amount. "But for now, they'll work."

With reluctance, Grayson picked up a brush, dipping it into a container of crimson-colored paint. It shouldn't have made him as nervous as he was. But as he swirled the brush around in the container, he couldn't help but feel like he'd be ruining something precious, something beautiful that only Sophia had the power to create.

With a gentle hand, he swiped a short stroke on the canvas, filling in the outlined rose with all the care and love it deserved. Maybe it wasn't perfect.

But as long as Sophia liked it, that was all that mattered.

"See, there's nothing to be nervous about," she said with a smile. "You're doing great."

Grayson smiled. "Maybe someday I'll have a fraction of the talent you have." He looked down at the container, then back to the table behind them. "I think I need a refill."

"All of the smaller tubes should be in that case on the far right."

Grayson hopped up and began digging through the case. With everything color-coded, finding the right red shade was a breeze.

Well, almost, anyway.

He popped open the cap, squeezing the life out of the tube as it sputtered nothing but air, then turned it so he could stare into the opening. Nothing appeared to be blocking the entrance, and the tube didn't feel empty.

But as he continued squeezing, a burst of red shot out, splattering his face and shirt. "Shit!"

So much for keeping his clothes clean.

Sophia's eyes snapped in his direction. "Are you okay?" she asked, jumping up to help. He turned, feeling embarrassed as hell as he stood and faced her. "Oh, shit!" Sophia laughed. "I'm so sorry. Let me go get a warm rag or something."

In a flash, she was back, insistent to come to his aid.

"Hold still," she said. "Luckily, the paint's fresh enough that it hasn't dried onto your skin." She leaned in, pressing the warm washcloth against his skin. With gentle strokes, the paint began to fade as she wiped at his skin, sending his pulse racing.

His jaw tensed. Being this close to her was torture.

Pure torture.

Yet, like a junkie, he was hooked.

Chapter

EIGHT

Even after another evening with Gray, Steve's words echoed through Sophia's mind. She couldn't help it. The worry was there, constantly screaming in the background. *Maybe Steve's right,* she thought. Maybe Gray wasn't who she thought he was.

But he couldn't be right. Gray hadn't done a single thing wrong, and he'd shown her nothing but kindness. If anything, he'd been nicer to her than most of the people she'd known in that town her entire life.

But still, she couldn't shake the feeling that something terrible was about to happen. The tension was there, heavy and electric in the air, like the sky just before a summer storm.

And something just didn't feel right.

She parked her car in the driveway and glanced over at Steve's house. His car was there; a sure sign that he would be in for the evening. Outside of work and class, he didn't have a life.

Well, other than checking in on you, apparently, she thought.

She guided her thoughts away from him. Just thinking about him was enough to make her cringe.

Her eyes drifted to his house once more. Not a soul was in the yard, but as her eyes scanned the property, she honed in on a figure standing in front of one of the windows upstairs.

A shudder rippled through her as her mind raced to the worst possible conclusion. Like clockwork, the little voice in her head was back, taunting her in the worst of ways.

Okay, just calm down, she thought. She took a deep breath. *Maybe it's not what you think it is.*

Still, the thought did nothing to steady her heart as it thudded against her ribcage. The thought of Steve spying on her, watching her every move was enough to make her sick.

And enough to make her pissed off beyond all belief.

What an asshole, she thought. *Does he really think I won't call him out on this bullshit?* Adrenaline rushed through her veins as she flung open the car door. Two could play this game.

And she wouldn't hesitate to get in his face.

Like a storm, she whirled into her house, feeling like she was on a warpath. All she had to do now was ditch her bag and go over and give him a piece of her mind.

"Everything okay, Sophia?" her mother shouted after her.

She let out an audible groan. "No. Our freaking neighbor's a creeping weirdo."

Her mother eyed her with disbelief. "I think you're being a little overdramatic."

"Seriously? Is it really that overdramatic when the guy literally stood at his window staring down at me?"

Her mother shook her head. Sophia's imagination always ran wild to a small extent. But *this?*

This was over the top.

"I think you're just a little paranoid, Sophia."

She threw her hands in the air. "I'm *not* being paranoid! Not to mention, he bugged me earlier this week because he wanted to grill me about Grayson."

Her mother eyed her suspiciously. "Okay, why don't you sit down, and we will talk about this. And while we're on the topic, what exactly is your status with Grayson?"

Yep. This is exactly what I was afraid of, Sophia thought. Of course, the minute she announced her status to the world, her mother would want to know every last detail about him down to his freaking blood type. Yeah, she knew this conversation would have to have to happen at some point.

But for God's sake, why did this have to come up now when she wasn't ready to deal with it?

"Mom, he's literally just a friend, okay? There's not much to really know."

Just a friend. Oh, she'd used that line so many times before when she'd been Sophia's age.

And she'd used it enough times to know that it was complete and utter bullshit.

Sophia slumped down in her chair. She didn't want to talk about Steve. The guy was a nutcase.

End of story.

Her mother shook her head, half-laughing at the silliness of the situation. "You know, your father used to stare out the window across the street from my house when I still lived at home. Did you ever stop to think that maybe Steve likes you?"

Sophia's head banged against the table, letting her hair splay out around her dramatically. "Yeah, but at least Dad wasn't a creep. Pretty sure you would never have dated him if he had been."

She laughed and nodded at her daughter. "You're right about that."

Sophia's stomach grumbled. She was starving, nearly on the verge of feeling edgy as she lifted her head, letting her hair cascade around her face. "I just don't know what to do. He acts like Grayson's the worst person to ever walk the face of the planet."

Her mother tossed her oven mitts off and sat down across from Sophia. "Could it be that he's jealous?"

Sophia sat in silence. It was one thing to have her own fears. But to have them echoed? That was borderline frightening.

And creepy.

"I think it's worth talking to him about it," she continued. "But don't go over there with a bunch of attitude. Guys never respond well to that."

She had a point. Not that it stopped her from feeling the anger boiling inside her. But her mother was right.

If she came out swinging, it would only end in disaster. She needed to give herself time.

Even if she didn't exactly want to.

"I don't know. I think I just need to cool down."

Sophia grabbed her bag and headed upstairs, feeling a faint vibration against her side as she walked into her room. No doubt, it was probably Cassie, wanting to know if she was free.

But secretly, she hoped it would be Gray instead.

She pulled her phone out, feeling ridiculously excited as she read Gray's name on the screen. But just as quickly as she became excited, the high had faded, leaving her with more questions than answers as her blood pounded furiously in her veins. She read the text again in disbelief.

Gotta leave for work soon, but someone slashed my damn tires. Can you give me a ride???

Sophia's heart slammed in her chest. God only knew why anyone would do something so shitty to him, but she was determined to get to the bottom of it. She quickly texted Grayson back.

Omg… Are you OK?

Panic set in as Grayson looked down at his phone. Yeah, what had happened was a big deal. But making Sophia freak out unnecessarily was the last thing he wanted to do. He fired back a quick response.

Yes, I'm OK. Will just need a ride tonight.

Sophia was still clinging to her phone when the next text came in. At least his message gave her some small relief now that she knew he was okay. But still.

Who would do this to him? Had he done something to piss someone off? She squeezed her eyes shut. Surely, there had to be some semi-rational explanation for this.

Relax, she thought. *It could've just been random vandalism.* But somehow, that just didn't seem to be the case. Something was making her Spidey-senses on high alert.

But *what?*

She typed back a quick response.

Be there ASAP.

With fear and anxiety propelling her forward, she tossed her phone into her bag and flew down the stairs, practically slamming into her Mom in the process.

"Hey are you going somewhere?" her mother asked. "Because I don't recall you asking."

Sophia cringed. Why couldn't she just have *normal* parents that didn't give a shit where she was going or what she was up to?

She rushed out the words, hoping if she blurted them out fast enough it would be enough to satisfy her mother. "It's kinda an emergency. I have to go pick up Grayson, or he'll be late to work."

Her mother opened her mouth to speak, but Sophia cut in, keeping any sort of rebuttal at bay.

"Mom, please. I'm eighteen, okay? I gotta hurry. Someone slashed his tires, and he doesn't exactly have anyone to turn to right now."

"Listen," she said, leaning against the railing, "I can appreciate you wanting to help, but I don't need all the attitude. I'm just trying to make sure I know what's going on in my daughter's life."

"I'll keep you in the loop, okay? Promise."

"Okay, okay, go. But be back by eleven, all right? I know it's not a school night, but you know nothing good ever happens after midnight."

"Thanks, Mom," she called.

She threw open the front door and practically sprinted to the car. Luckily for her, she'd already committed the directions to Grayson's house to memory. It wasn't exactly the *closest* place nearby, but as long as there were no cops on those back roads…

She could push it.

Yeah, it wouldn't be the *wisest* idea, but she could push it.

She cranked the radio in her car, letting the opening guitar riff of *Be My Escape* fill the air. Maybe it was a coincidence, or maybe it was fate. But Grayson was the escape she'd needed for so long. And no matter how fast she had to drive, she'd get there.

Because as crazy as it seemed,
she was already starting to feel like she'd do
anything for him.

Chapter
NINE

Even as upset as Grayson was, he couldn't help but feel relieved as Sophia pulled up. She was a godsend in so many ways. Everyone in his family had noticed a change in him, and it was hard to deny that she had the power to lift him out of the darkest mood.

Grayson's mother peeked out at the two of them from the living room window, watching as her son climbed inside Sophia's car. Of course, being a parent, she wasn't privy to every thought and every feeling her children had. All three of them were beyond the phase where they told her every last detail of their lives.

But it was plain as day to see that Grayson was absolutely, one-hundred percent head-over-heels with the girl. He didn't have to say it.

It was etched all over his face.

Sophia put the car in reverse, letting it quickly roll down the driveway as Grayson fumbled with his seatbelt. "Thanks again," he said. "I really didn't think I'd be able to make it to work tonight."

Sophia smiled, keeping her eyes focused on the road ahead of her. "No worries. I'll get you there in no time."

"Just don't take off out of here like a bat outta hell. I don't need my Mom getting pissed."

Sophia stifled a laugh. "I can't even imagine your mom getting mad. She's always so chill."

"Trust me, she can get mad. Not usually with me, though. Usually, it's Brian that she gets pissed at."

She let out an audible sigh. "Oh, the things I miss out on by not having siblings! I'm sure it's never a dull moment around your house." She looked over, noticing Gray squirming in his seat like an inchworm. "What the heck are you doing?"

Grayson lifted himself from the seat and pulled his phone from his pocket. "Trying to fish this out," he said, holding up his phone. "Have no idea who the hell would be texting me right now."

"Maybe it's someone from work?"

Gray stared at the screen in disbelief. "Okay… I guess I'm not alone in this fight," he mumbled.

She glanced over at him, noticing the scowl on his face. "What's *that* supposed to mean?"

Gray ran a hand through his hair. At least some of the pressure was off now, though it still didn't explain why he'd been targeted. Then again, did *any* criminal ever need a reason to cause trouble?

And he sure as hell didn't know how to feel about the text he'd just received.

"It was a news alert. I guess there looking to see if anyone has any tips about who's been vandalizing shit."

Sophia's mind swirled in a thousand directions. There was only one person she could possibly think of that could be behind it all, but suspicions wouldn't be enough. She needed proof.

Cold, hard, *undeniable* proof.

And by God, sooner rather than later, she was going to get it.

Gray paused for a moment, feeling something in his heart settle in place as he Sophia finally came to a stop. What he was beginning to feel for her was something far bigger than he ever thought possible. And though he didn't know how to fully explain it, one word flashed over and over again in his mind like a neon sign.

Love.

Snapshots of the future flickered in his mind. He'd never thought that far ahead, even with his own life, but now that Sophia was here, things were just… different. A whirlwind. Chaos.

And he loved every minute.

Funny how one single, four-letter word had the power to turn everything inside out, unlocking doors to emotions he never thought possible. And now that the doors were opened, he never wanted them to close.

He leaned in, pressing a soft, gentle kiss to her lips. He'd been waiting for this moment for so long that it almost didn't register that it was happening. It was really, truly happening. And he never wanted it to end.

"Thanks again," he whispered. "I'll call you tonight when I get out."

The next few moments were nothing short of a blur as Sophia's world flipped upside down onto its head. *He kissed me. He actually kissed me.* A slow smile spread across her face.

Maybe for once, her wishes were finally coming true after all.

The high Sophia had quickly faded as she pulled into her driveway, only to find Steve standing at her front door talking to her mom. Of all the places that arrogant asshole could've been, and he chose this night and this moment to come crawling up to her doorstep. *Some luck,* she thought. *God only knows what the hell is doing here.* The very thought made her cringe. Whatever this was about couldn't possibly be good.

At the sound of her car door opening, Steve turned to look at her, staring at her with cold eyes. It certainly hadn't been the first time he'd looked at her that way.

And it probably wouldn't be the last.

She stormed out of her car and charged up the sidewalk. Judging by the look on her mother's face, the conversation wasn't going well, and now that Sophia had arrived, there wasn't any doubt in her mind that this evening was going to be an absolute shit-show.

"I'm surprised you're over here," Sophia snapped. "Figured you would've preferred to stare over here from the comfort of your own home, instead."

Steve's face went white as a bedsheet. "What the hell are you talking about?"

Her eyes darted to her mother, standing frozen like a statue as her daughter tore into the poor kid.

"I saw you, okay? You don't have to act like you weren't spying because I've already caught you. More than once, actually. And I don't know what the hell your problem is, but fix it. Because *my* business isn't *yours.*"

"Sophia, honey, I—"

Sophia cut her mother off. "You just can't stop defending him, can you, Mom? I mean, really! Whose side are you on?"

"Honey, he was just trying to see if it had started snowing yet."

Snowing? Yeah, freaking right. Like anyone would buy that line of total crap.

"You're joking, right?" she asked, turning to Steve. "That's the best you could come up with?"

"It's the truth," he said coldly. "And as far as the other night goes, I'm sorry you don't want to listen to me. But you have to believe me."

Sophia let out a laugh. "Trust me. That's *never* going to happen."

She pushed past both of them, making a beeline for the stairs. They could sit there and babble at each other all they wanted, but she was done with both of them for the evening, and there wasn't a damn thing that would change her mind about Steve. He was nothing short of certifiable at this point.

And she was thoroughly sick and tired of his bullshit.

She locked her door behind her and flopped down on her bed, staring at the ceiling in exasperation. With any luck, her mom might just leave her the hell alone for the rest of the evening.

And as far as she was concerned, that would be just fine.

Chapter

TEN

With a half-hearted laugh, Cassie strolled up to Sophia's locker first thing Monday morning. "So, did you blow up at Steve over the weekend or something? He seems to be in a mood."

Sophia rolled her eyes. "Yeah, well, apparently he thinks he needs to lecture my mom about all the reasons why I shouldn't be around Grayson. Not that he's bothered to tell *me* what those reasons are."

"That's so freaking weird. I mean, why exactly does he give a shit so much about what you do?"

Sophia burst into laughter at the sight of Cassie's contorted face. "Because he's a possessive nutcase? I don't know. I swear, the guy has all the makings of being a serial killer."

Cassie nearly spat out her water. "God, I can almost picture that. That's scary."

"Tell me about it. I'm half afraid I'll wake up one night and he'll be standing in the corner of my room."

"Well," Cassie said, "at least your bedroom window doesn't face his house."

Sophia sighed as she adjusted her bag on her shoulder. "Still doesn't make me feel that great, though. But at least when I move, I won't have to deal with him anymore."

"If he doesn't hunt you down and take you out first," Cassie snickered.

Sophia gave her a playful shove, half-joking yet feeling half-terrified at the thought. "You'd better hope that doesn't happen."

"I hope not. I don't really know what I'd do without you."

"Well, I know you wouldn't date Grayson," Sophia laughed. "So, at least *that's* a weight off my shoulders."

"Damn right. If I have to hear another word about freaking history or science, my eyes are gonna roll back into my head." Cassie stopped just outside of her next period class. "And speaking of Gray, let me guess, you're going to busy with him this weekend again?"

"Not all weekend, but Saturday, yeah. I'm meeting his grandma for the first time."

"That sounds…" Cassie's voice trailed off. "Interesting?"

"It will be. I'm actually kinda excited. And nervous."

"Why?" Cassie scoffed. "She's old. What's there to be nervous about?"

Everything, she thought. She'd never reached this stage with any guy before. This would be a whole new experience.

And it didn't matter that the woman was eighty years old. She wanted to start things off on the right foot.

"Um, everything. I want her to like me, Cass. She means a lot to him."

"Just be yourself. You'll be fine." Cassie pulled out her phone and checked the time. "Shit, I gotta get in there. Wanna meet at Clem's after class?"

Sophia shook her head. "I can't. I'm heading to Gray's afterward."

Cassie rolled her eyes. "Fine. But who passes up caffeine?"

Me, Sophia thought. She didn't need a caramel macchiato to put a little extra spring in her step.

Because Grayson Cawthorne was doing a pretty fine job of that all by himself.

With her back aching from the weight of her backpack, Sophia trudged her way to her car, feeling every last ache and pain along the way. It had been a long day, but even as exhausted as she felt, that little silver lining she'd been daydreaming about all day had been all the motivation she needed to keep going.

Yes, a movie night was just what the doctor ordered. It didn't matter that they were about a thousand years past Halloween. They were having a scary movie night in the dead of winter.

But at least now, she had the perfect snuggling partner to go along with it.

She let out a sigh of relief as she opened her car door. A little popcorn, a little horror, and a whole lot of cuddling.

Yeah, that was the perfect recipe for the perfect night.

Sophia smiled. She could practically smell the popcorn popping to life on the stove. Gray said there was nothing better than a movie night with some old-fashioned popcorn.

And truth be told, he was right. Some things really were better back in the day.

Like the comfort of a warm blanket, pulling into Grayson's driveway felt like coming home. And in a way, it was home, at least, where her heart was concerned.

Grayson stared from the window, waiting in anticipation as Sophia made her way to the front door. At least tonight wouldn't end like it had the night before. It still sucked beyond all belief that his car was a complete disaster, and God only knew how long it would take to save up for all four tires.

But as shitty as the situation was, it could've been worse.

Much worse.

Except, the string of bad luck never seemed to stop coming to the doorstep of the Cawthorne household.

"Everything okay?" Sophia asked as she walked through the door.

His jaw tensed as he pulled a wrinkled piece of paper from his pocket. "I found this in my locker right before I left for the day."

Goosebumps formed on the back of Sophia's neck as she read the words aloud. "Your sister's next." She pressed her palm to her mouth. "I just don't understand. It's like someone has it out for everyone in this town."

Gray remained silent, though his gaze lingered on Sophia as she pulled off her coat and tossed it on the couch. The less time he spent dwelling on the situation, the better off he would be.

And thank God Sophia was there to distract him.

"Do you want me to take that for you?" he asked.

Sophia smiled. Even facing a whirlwind of chaos, he was so sweet. So kind. And so much of everything she ever wanted. She nodded. "You can if you want."

"Well, sure, it's no problem. I mean, at least this way it will dry faster."

She settled down on the couch, unraveling the throw blanket that had been piled on the other end. She had been chilled to the bone—not only from the freezing cold but from the fear that was growing inside her.

Was this what Steve meant when he said Gray wasn't the type of guy she should be hanging with?

She brushed the thought aside. It couldn't be, and that nagging idiot needed to get out of her head and out of her business.

A few minutes passed before Grayson returned plopped a giant bowl of popcorn between them. "I figured we could share."

Sophia smiled as she snuggled further down into the blanket. "Deal. Do you want some of the blanket?"

"Nah," he said, popping a kernel in his mouth, "I'm good. But thank you."

"So, what's on our watch list for tonight?"

"*Drag Me to Hell.* Which, from what I've heard, it's not even that scary. Plus, it's only rated PG-13."

"So? I get scared shitless over anything. But I like scary movies."

"That's so weird," he laughed. "I mean, how do you like something that freaks you out?"

She thought about it for a moment. "I dunno. The adrenaline rush, I guess. And it's an excuse to cuddle."

Grayson laughed. "So, that's the *real* reason why. I see how it is." He grabbed another fistful of popcorn. "I guess we'll have to watch scary movies more often."

Thirty minutes into the movie, Sophia's eyes were growing heavy, struggling to stay open as she cuddled against Grayson's arm.

"You're not falling asleep, are you?" he whispered.

"Nope," she yawned. "Just resting my eyes."

Grayson smiled as he gently threaded his fingers through her hair. She looked like an angel as she sat curled up against him.

And truth be told, she was the closest thing to heaven that he'd ever known. It didn't matter what else was going on in his world.

All that mattered was that Sophia Hillcrest was in his arms.

Sophia woke with a start. At first, she thought she was still at home, tucked away in her own bed. But a quick glance at her phone told her that not only had the movie completely passed her by, but she was going to be late.

Very late.

"Shit!" she cried. "Shit, shit, shit!" With her heart pounding furiously in her chest, she tossed her half of the blanket aside and scrambled to her feet.

Grayson stirred, feeling as though he was still lost in a hazy dream. "Soph?"

"I'm so sorry," she said frantically. "I didn't realize what time it was."

Grayson wiped the sleep from his eyes, then looked at the clock. "Oh, damn. Yeah, I guess it is late."

She grabbed her bag and fumbled with her coat, desperately wishing the zipper would cooperate for once. "Yeah, and they're going to kill me."

"Just for staying out late?"

"Yeah! It's a freaking school night! You're lucky you don't have to deal with this shit."

Grayson bolted to the door, capturing her hand in his as he pulled her into his arms. "Okay, well good night," he said, pressing a kiss to her lips. "Drive safe. Text me later."

She tossed her bag into the front seat, barely sitting down before turning the key in the ignition. *Five minutes.* If she floored it all the way there, she might be able to make it in time.

Maybe.

A few blown stop signs later, and she was right back home, safe and sound by the saving grace of something nothing more than a miracle. Just as she suspected, the lights were off in the living room. More than likely, her parents were already upstairs getting ready to head to bed. And that was all the more reason to be as quiet as a mouse, as she tiptoed up the stairs.

"Glad to see you know how to read a clock," her father sneered.

A jolt of adrenaline shot through her, making her freeze in place as he confronted her in the darkness. "I'm sorry. I lost track of time."

"Yeah, well, when we tell you to be back in this house by eleven, that doesn't you show up at 11:02."

"I'm sorry," she repeated. "I'll try to pay more attention."

"It's not a matter of trying," her father said. "It's a matter of *doing*. And if you want to be treated like an adult, then act like one."

With a heavy sigh, he turned and headed back up the stairs, leaving Sophia to stand there frozen. *This can't happen again,* she thought. She'd be lucky if they didn't ground her indefinitely, and that was something she couldn't stomach.

Because if she had to go without seeing Grayson, there would be hell to pay.

Chapter
ELEVEN

By the time the weekend arrived, the choppy waters had all but settled at Sophia's house, though her anxiety coursed through her more and more the closer Saturday came. It was one thing to make his mom happy. But this was a huge step.

And she couldn't afford to blow it.

Nervous energy thrummed through Sophia as she stood by Gray's side and waited for Grams to appear at the door. Maybe to the rest of the world, meeting someone's extended family for the first time wasn't that big of a deal. But to her, it was important. She wanted them to love her just as much as she loved Grayson.

Love. The word seized hold of her so fast it nearly took her breath away as she stood in front of Lillian Osbourne's door. Was this *that* what she was starting to feel? Love?

For a moment she went dizzy. Maybe it was. It wasn't like she'd ever cared for another human being the way she cared for him. To Sophia, the world began and ended at his feet. And she'd do anything to keep him forever.

The door finally opened, and a short, white-haired woman came into view. With thick, dark, penciled-in eyebrows, bright red lipstick, and jewelry for days, Lillian appeared every bit as artsy as Gray had described.

Lillian's mouth stood agape as her eyes locked on Gray's. "Oh, honey, I wasn't expecting you to come over today," she said, opening the front door.

Grayson exchanged a look with Sophia. Of course, he'd told Grams of his plans earlier in the week. But she didn't remember. In fact, he was lucky she even remembered who he was at all. *Thank God,* he thought. *At least she appears to be having a slightly good day.*

"Did you bring a friend?" she asked.

"Girlfriend, actually," he said, his cheeks heating. "But yeah, this is my girlfriend, Sophia."

Sophia extending her hand, taking Lillian's tiny, frail hand in hers. "So nice to finally meet you. Gray talks about you all the time."

Mixed with the smell of potpourri and something burnt, the annoyingly strong scent hit Grayson and Sophia's noses as they stepped inside, and Gray closed the door softly behind them as Lillian shuffled her way to the kitchenette. Sophia looked around, her eyes lighting up as she took in the numerous paintings and photographs on the walls. Her home wasn't a fancy place. Not by a long shot.

But for the time being, the facility would have to do. It was only temporary.

Or at least, that's what everyone in Gray's family had told themselves.

With a spatula that looked about as old as Lillian was, she scooped a pile of completely burnt cookies on a plate and placed it on the counter. "I think I left them in there a little long!" she laughed. "Hope you like them a little more crispy."

Grayson remained silent as sadness settled in his chest. There wasn't anything funny about the situation, and he had a sneaky suspicion she'd completely forgotten the oven was even on.

And *that* was a scary thought.

Lillian shuffled her way back into the tiny living area. "Feel free to sit wherever you'd like."

Sophia and Gray sat side by side on the couch, watching as the tiny woman shrank to nothing in her oversized recliner. The chair had seen better days, but it would be the last thing on Earth she parted with.

Grayson sighed. Even to this day, the sight of her in his grandfather's chair was a little heartbreaking. God, he missed the old days, when life was simpler. He'd give anything to go back.

Anything except give up Sophia.

"Tell me about yourself, Sophia," Lillian asked. "I want to hear all about you."

Gray looked down at Sophia's hand, resting gently against her leg. It would be so easy to reach out and take her hand in his. Someday he wanted to live to be Gram's age. But he wanted Sophia by his side, and he craved to touch her, to tell her exactly how he felt.

And yeah, maybe the world was a scary, unforgiving place at times, but as long as Sophia was by his side, he could take on the world.

And then some.

Chapter

TWELVE

Early Februrary

The snow fell silently as Sophia turned the key in her ignition to head home. After four and a half hours working of staring out into a nearly empty store, she was exhausted beyond belief. Her feet were aching, and truth be told, her heart was aching, too. Between school and work, and in particular, Grayson's ever-expanding work schedule, time was growing scarcer by the minute.

She blew into her hands, hoping the warmth would be enough to take the dull ache away. If Grayson had been there, he could've held them and warmed them back to life. But as she sat in the nearly empty parking lot, her heart sagged.

Yeah, making money was great, but it wasn't like she made that much, anyway. And now that the holiday rush was over, standing around waiting for customers to walk into Martelli's was like watching paint dry. She would've much rather spent the evening with Grayson.

Even if all they did was sit up in his room and talk.

She let out a sigh. Even if *she* would've been off work, the odds of him being off at the same time would've been virtually zero. Pizza Palace had been slammed as of late.

Or at least, ever since Mancini's rat fiasco.

Of course, things had been on the upswing for Pizza Palace *before* then. But as soon as the health department caught wind of the mess going on at Mancini's, practically everyone in town had jumped ship, leaving Pizza Palace to fill the void.

And in truth, the busy nights hadn't been *all* bad for the two of them. With the onslaught of business, Gray had replaced his tires in no time.

But some nights, Gray hadn't even come home until well after midnight. And sure, it made the time fly by, and he was able to bring home a little extra cash. But what good was that when they couldn't spend hardly any time together?

She rested her head against the steering wheel, wishing the tears forming in her eyes would disappear. Why did everything have to be so complicated?

And why did it have to feel like she was being stabbed in the chest every second they were apart? She sat up, wiping her eyes with the puffy sleeve of her coat. She needed to get it together.

But, still, every moment spent away from each other was precious time they would never get back, no matter how hard they tried.

Her tires spun slowly as she made her way down the main aisle, leaving the half-lit Martelli's sign behind in her rearview mirror. She mumbled under her breath. Of course, the plow people weren't going to bother with the snow until it was done for the night, but driving through it was a bitch in such a low-profile car, and at the rate she was going, she'd be lucky if she made it home by midnight herself.

Sophia let out an audible groan. Maybe someday the two of them would run away off into the sun, leaving this life behind. Yeah, it wasn't a perfect plan.

But what plan ever was?

Sophia's knuckles tensed as she gripped her steering wheel. The combination of snow and sleet made for a treacherous drive, and even though her phone kept vibrating in her bag, she kept her hands frozen in place, resisting the temptation to respond. Grayson could wait. Didn't change the fact that her hands itched to reply.

But he could wait.

Nearly an hour later, Sophia finally made the turn down her street. Flashing red and blue lights reflected off the houses, and she squinted into the darkness, trying to make out which house the cops were at. If she didn't know any better…

She blinked furiously, wondering if her eyes were playing tricks on her. The cops appeared to be at *her* house.

But *why?*

A surge of panic shot through her veins. Nothing about this made sense.

And maybe it hadn't been Grayson texting her, after all.

Sophia parked in the street, watching from her car as the lights shut off on the first squad car and pulled out of the driveway. Her parents, both shellshocked and horrified, stood in the driveway, desperately waiting to see her, and when at last the second squad car left, Sophia charged up the driveway, trudging through the snow. Her eyes widened as they zeroed in on the living room window, completely shattered beyond all belief.

"What the hell happened?" she cried. "Are you guys okay?"

"We're fine," her father said. "There's been a break-in, but we are okay. No one got hurt."

Tears stung at Sophia's eyes. "A break-in?" she squeaked. "Why the hell would someone do this to us?"

Her mother shook her head. "I don't know, honey. I don't know." Hot tears rained down her cheeks. "I'm just glad the worthless bastard left the hammer they used behind."

Smart criminal, Sophia thought sarcastically. At least the asshole might actually get caught, then.

Provided they had a record, at least.

"There's a good chance whoever did this is the same person who's been behind the other vandalism," her father said.

A wave of nausea settled in Sophia's stomach. All she wanted right now was for Gray to hold her in his arms and tell her everything was going to be okay.

Even if they both knew that wasn't the truth.

Her vocal cords tightened as she tried to choke out her words. "How are we supposed to feel safe again?"

Her father wrapped an arm around her shoulder, squeezing her tight. "We'll get there. It will just take some time."

Chapter
THIRTEEN

Valentine's Day

From the moment Sophia's eyes opened, she could hardly wait for seven o'clock to roll around. For once, Valentine's Day wasn't going to suck; a statement she could never have said any other year of her life. But this year was different.

And for once, she actually had a reason to care.

She rolled over, sending Gray a quick text before she rolled out of bed.

Ready for our date tonight?

She was ready. *Beyond* ready.

And now she just needed the next twelve hours to go by in a flash.

Dancing on her tiptoes, she bounced down the stairs, feeling as light as a feather. Somehow, the coffee and pancakes smelled sweeter today.

But wasn't *everything* supposed to be sweeter on this day?

Her mother glanced over her shoulder as Sophia bounded into the kitchen. "Morning, Soph." She poured herself a cup of coffee, smiling to herself as her daughter bounded into the kitchen. She remembered what that was like, when everything was new and exciting, flying by at a million miles an hour. *Oh, to be that age but have the wisdom I have now,* she thought. "Are you excited about your date tonight?"

Sophia's eyes lit up. "Yeah. I just wish I didn't have to sit through class for a million years first, though," she said. "What about you? Are you excited for your little getaway weekend?"

Her mother smiled. "Of course. Your father and I haven't been anywhere in ages." She took a swig of her coffee. "It'll be nice."

Sophia grabbed her bag from the counter and headed toward the door.

"Be careful tonight," her mother called after her. "And be smart."

Sophia rolled her eyes. Parents could just be so damn awkward at times. "Yeah, Mom, love you too. Thanks for the much-needed advice," she called.

Sophia squinted as she opened the front door. Like usual, the air was crisp, but for once, the sun had made an appearance, bringing with it the promise of a good day ahead. A *really* good day ahead.

And her mood did not go unnoticed.

As always, Cassie was at Sophia's locker, but today Cassie had a grin like she'd won the lottery. And judging by the look on Sophia's face, she was having a pretty damn good day, too.

"Well, *you're* in a good mood," Sophia said. "Did you finally score a date with Skyler?"

Cassie rolled her eyes. "No, but I think this is even better. Well, at least for *you.*" She held her phone up to Sophia's face. "Guess who got busted!"

Sophia's eyes grew wide as saucers as she scanned the headline on the screen.

Police ID suspect in recent break-ins, vandalism

Sophia read it again, studying the mugshot on the screen.

No. There was no way it could possibly be him. She couldn't get that lucky.

Could she?

"Is that…"

"Yep!" Cassie squealed. "It's freaking Steve!"

"Holy shit. Wow. I mean, I can't say I'm surprised. He's been weirder than usual lately."

Cassie nodded. "Yeah, and get this. He had several pounds of dope on him when they caught him. So, it looks like you're
not gonna have to deal with him for a while."

"Yeah, and at least I won't have to worry about him staring out the window at me, either."

♥♥♥

The night had been nothing short of perfect.

It didn't matter that it wasn't their first date. Or their second. Or their third. This night would always be a special night.

And one that they would never forget.

With weary legs, Sophia bumbled out of the car, swaying as she raised her arms high over her head. Yeah, she could barely stay upright, she was so tired.

But damn, it felt good to get out and stretch.

"Easy now," Grayson said. "Don't need you falling flat on your face."

She let out a small laugh. "I'm fine. I just need some sleep." Time stood still as her hand hovered over the doorknob. It was a strange feeling to come home to an empty house. Not to mention it had been *years* since Sophia's parents had gone away for any decent length of time. And now, with the house all to herself, there was something slightly eerie about it. "Can you come in with me?" she asked. "I hate walking in by myself when nobody's home."

Grayson's brows lifted. "I think someone's been watching too many horror flicks."

"Something like that." Sophia reached for his hands and begged like a small child. "Pretty please? I know it's late, but you could always stay the night. If you wanted to, that is."

Grayson's heart thudded in his chest. There was nothing he wanted more than to wake up with her in his arms. "I will if you want me to."

Sophia reached up, wrapping her arms around Grayson's neck. "I do."

"Consider it done, then." Grayson crushed his lips to hers, eager to taste every corner of mouth until she begged for more. He'd been waiting for this from the moment he'd arrived earlier in the evening to pick her up. And now, he couldn't take it anymore. He was practically crawling out of his skin, desperate to kiss every inch of her. He wanted her all to himself, uninterrupted.

And for once, he was finally going to get his wish.

"We better go inside," she whispered.

"I know. Or we'll never make it into the house."

Taking her hand, he took the lead and pushed the front door open, fumbling for the light switch.

"Oh, God, I'm freaking blind now," she whined, shielding her eyes. "Warn a girl next time."

Grayson couldn't help but laugh. "Well, how else are we supposed to find our way around? By flashlight?"

"Maybe," she groaned. "Well, at least I'm wide awake now. So, thanks for that."

The cold hardwood floor felt freezing against Sophia's feet as she kicked off her boots and padded her way to the kitchen. With a flop, she plunked her purse down on the counter and shrugged her coat off, feeling the full effect of the cool air as it touched her skin.

"Aren't you cold?" he asked. "I can load some wood in the fireplace if you want."

Her teeth practically chattered as she spoke. "That would be amazing," she said. "I don't think the damn furnace is working."

With a huff, she marched over to it, squinting at the display. *Shit. Well, this is going to be a miserable weekend.*

Not to mention her parents would be pissed. Things like that weren't exactly cheap to replace around the house.

She let out an exasperated sigh. "Nope, it's not working," she called.

Silence filled the room, and Sophia peeked around the corner, only to realize Grayson had already headed out to bring in the firewood.

She smiled to herself. If he was any sweeter, she'd be in a freaking sugar coma for sure.

With Grayson off and running, she made her way upstairs, feeling only a tiny bit warmer as she reached the top step. She rubbed her hands across her arms. It could be the coldest day of the year, but somehow, just the thought of his arms around her was enough to warm her body and heart.

She tugged at the tie around her neck, letting her dress fall to the floor in a heap, and with the moonlight streaming into her room, she gazed at her reflection in the mirror, noticing the way the moonlight danced against her arms and legs. She'd never been comfortable in her own skin.

At least, not until Gray came along.

He loved every part of her, every angle, every side, and his love gave her all the confidence in the world. She could achieve anything as long as he believed in her.

And by God, he would never stop believing in her for as long as they both lived.

She pulled the old Pizza Palace shirt he'd given her from her drawer. It didn't matter that it was way too big and way too baggy to possibly be *hers*. She loved that damn thing, and even if it got holes or stains, it would always be her favorite. She would always cherish it.

Her thoughts drifted to Gray. She'd never shared a bed even with a friend before, much less someone she was in a relationship with.

She swallowed hard. Maybe he was just as nervous as she was.

She'd wanted this for so long, but still, the thought was nerve racking, sending little butterflies fluttering in her stomach. There would be no going back from this. They would be forever tied from this point forward.

She quickly brushed her teeth then fumbled around the bathroom drawer, hoping to find her dental floss, but as her hand reached all the way to the back of the drawer, her heart sank. *Shit.*

So much for *that* idea.

"Soph?"

She jumped in place, half-startled by his voice. "I'm in the bathroom. I'll be out in a second."

Sophia looked down at underwear, suddenly feeling awkward about the pink stars printed on them. So, they weren't the cutest pair from Victoria's Secret. Big deal. Would that really matter? Would Gray even notice at all?

Doubtful. Half the time, guys were dense as hell.

"Everything okay?" he called.

Another shot of adrenaline soared through her. "Yeah, I'll be right there."

With the light off, she emerged from the bathroom quietly, and Gray sat on the edge of the bed in silence, drinking her in as she came into view. God help him, there was something undeniably hot about her wearing his shirt.

"I'm sorry," she said. "I probably look like trash."

Gray shook his head. "You could never look like trash." His arms reached for her, begging her to come closer. "Come here."

She sat down beside him, feeling the heat radiating from his chest. "You know we don't have to do this if you don't want to."

He turned to her, brushing a few wayward strands of hair from her face, and pressed his forehead to hers. "Trust me," he panted. "I want to. Just as badly as you do."

Time stood still as their lips hovered near each other. They were on the precipice, dangerously close to falling off the edge. But if there ever was a time to take the plunge into the unknown, it was right here, right now.

Her arms wrapped around his neck, pulling him in tightly as their lips crashed together in a heated fury, and desperate hunger took hold as their tongues feverishly met each other stroke for stroke. Sophia was in a haze now, kissing him greedily as though it was the last night she'd ever have with him. He tasted like sweetness and cinnamon, and as she lost herself to his kiss, she knew she would never want anyone else but him. No matter how much the last several months felt like a dream, they were real. He was real.

And she never wanted this night to end.

She settled herself in his lap, and he pulled her closer, letting his hands trace the outlines of her curves from underneath the thin cotton shirt. Maybe she was sexy as hell in it, but it would look even better if it was on the floor, and a soft cry escaped her as his fingertips skimmed her skin, tracing a path down to the waistband of her underwear. She inhaled deeply, feeling his fingers tease her as they hovered over the fabric.

"Are you absolutely sure about this?" he asked.

"Yes," she breathed. "Yes, I've never been more sure about anything."

Grayson scooped her up in his arms, letting her settle softly against the mattress as his lips grazed her jawline. Every part of her was perfect, and even if it took all night to kiss every part of her, he would do it.

They had nothing but time.

And if the world stopped spinning some time in the distant future, at least they would always have each other.

The End

For more great romance reads, visit
nicolehighlandwrites.com

New Adult

Sweetest Love Trilogy
Diving Right In (Crescent Key, 1)
Splashing Right In (Crescent Key, 2)
Business and Pleasure
Furever in Love

Paranormal

Darkest Temptation (Vampires of Somerset, 1)
Forever My Valentine
Claimed: An Alien Abduction Short Story

Fantasy

Diamond in the Night

Historical

With Every Kiss (Somershire Chronicles, 1)
Her Every Wish (Somershire Chronicles, 2)

Holiday

Her Christmas Wish
One Very Merry Night

To stay current with the latest news & more, sign up for Nicole's mailing list!

Receive
Sweetest Kiss
for free when
you sign up!

<u>Sign up</u> today!

About

NICOLE

Nicole Highland is a fiction author from Fort Wayne, Indiana. Having her start as a romance writer, she knows life doesn't always give us a happy ending, so that's why she creates her own.

Highland writes romances featuring a bit of heat, and a whole helping of sweet, and prefers her heroes to be on the softer side and love to open doors for their ladies. She is the author of more than ten different novellas and writes new adult, paranormal, fantasy, and historical romances. In addition to writing fiction, she loves writing free-verse poetry.

When she's not writing, she's most likely using her creativity in some other fashion, and she currently works full time as a graphic designer and does freelance design work and writing in her spare time.

Thank You

FOR READING!

www.ingramcontent.com/pod-product-compliance
Lightning Source LLC
Chambersburg PA
CBHW071958150726
47999CB00001B/481